LIONHEART

If you enjoy reading this book,
you might like to try another story
from the **MAMMOTH READ** series:

LIONHEART

Lynne Markham

illustrated by

CHRIS CHAPMAN

mammoth

For Robert and Ben,
with love
L.M.

For Ross,
with love
C.C.

First published in Great Britain in 1998 by Mammoth
an imprint of Reed International Books Limited
Michelin House, 81 Fulham Road, London SW3 6RB

Text copyright © 1998 Lynne Markham
Illustrations copyright © 1998 Chris Chapman

The rights of Lynne Markham and Chris Chapman to be
identified as the author and illustrator of this work have
been asserted by them in accordance with the
Copyright, Designs and Patents Act 1988

ISBN 0 7497 3405 1

10 9 8 7 6 5 4 3 2 1

A CIP catalogue record for this book is
available from the British Library

Printed in Great Britain by Cox & Wyman Ltd,
Reading, Berkshire

Contents

1 The lion on the wall

FOR AS LONG as he could remember, Leo had wanted to be a lion. In his room there were cats everywhere. They sprawled over every inch of wall. There were cheetahs and

pumas and a couple of tigers, and a leopard up in a tree with its prey. But his favourite picture was of a lion. The lion stood alone on an African plain. In the picture the sun was shining; it picked out the strands of the lion's pelt and turned them into flaming gold.

Sometimes, if it was very quiet, Leo thought he could hear the lion breathe. Its eyes seemed to follow him round the room. Once Leo thought he had heard it roar. That was the day Kevin Phipps stole his lunch. Kevin was bigger and older than Leo. He pushed Leo up against a wall. 'Give us your lunch *or else*!' he said. When Leo tried to push him away he said, 'Give over, stupid – you're much too small!'

Leo told the lion everything when he got home and the lion seemed to understand. When Leo told him about Kevin Phipps, the lion appeared suddenly bigger and darker. A black shadow skimmed across his eyes and Leo was certain he heard a deep rumbling roar.

Sometimes Leo roared himself. But he did it quietly in his room. He roared at his brother Sean for teasing him about being so small, and he roared at Kevin for stealing his lunch and at the teacher who had once made him stand on his chair when he didn't manage to finish his sums. When Leo roared the lion roared back, but silently, as if he was playing.

Now Leo climbed on to his bed and lay

on his back with his head on his hands. He stared at the lion blazing out from the wall. He thought about his grandad who had lived in Africa among the leopards and lions and heard them roar through the dense, dark night.

Grandad was a bit of a stranger to Leo – mostly because he lived so far away. He

had not seen Leo since he was very small
and Leo was rather afraid of him. He
remembered his grandad as huge and
brown, with a lot of very long white hair.
When Grandad spoke his voice was a
roar. 'Who's this?' he roared when he first
met Leo. 'Leo? Well, well! Another one,
eh? Another chip off the Leopold block.
Well, lad, I suppose you're named after
me.' He had stared at Leo very closely,
and his eyes were a fierce, tawny yellow
under his bushy brows. When he finished
his stare he nodded slowly. 'Aye,' he said,

'I reckon you'll do.' And his voice was suddenly soft and low – almost a growl, Leo remembered now. He had leaned down close to Leo's head. 'You've a great heart inside you, lad,' he said. 'See you remember that when things get tough.'

After that Grandad had straightened up and boomed across to Leo's mum, 'Look after this lad, Evie, d'you hear? He'll be carrying on the Leopold line.'

Leo thought about what Grandad had said – about him having a great heart in his chest. But how could that be when he was so small? Had Grandad meant it as a joke? Leo closed his eyes to shut out the lion. He conjured up a picture of Grandad's face, and Grandad seemed to be laughing at him. His mouth was open and his head was thrown back. The white hair tossed about his face. But the laugh was catching, and Leo laughed back.

Next week he would meet Grandad again. He would ask him what he meant by the laugh, and by saying that Leo had a special heart. Grandad was a puzzle to Leo. He was kind and fierce at the same time. He wasn't like anyone else Leo knew. He was grander, more frightening – and somehow more wild.

2 **The lion and Grandad**

LEO'S GRANDAD LIVED alone. To get to his house you had to go down a lane, through a gate, and down another narrower lane. Then you had to leave the car and go down a path that was overgrown. At the end of this path was Grandad's house.

Going up the path to Grandad's door was like going through a jungle. Twisted roots prised up the ground and skeins of leaves blocked out the light. His door-knocker was a giant lion's head. Leo's dad said to his mum, 'Why can't he live somewhere sensible? I mean, what would happen if he was ill?'

'Dad's never ill,' said Leo's mum. 'He's strong as an ox and always has been. He's just a bit slower than he was before.'

Leo knocked at the door with the lion's head, and from deep in the house they could hear Grandad yell, 'Hang on, will you? Shan't be a tick – can't find the key to the blasted door!'

After that they heard him shout again, 'Got it! Under the biscuit tin!' Then the key rattled in the old-fashioned lock.

When the door opened Grandad stood in the gap. His body filled up the whole of the space; he was bigger and brighter and more magnificent than Leo remembered. His hair gleamed silver with threads of gold, his beard thrust out from his face like spears, and at his throat was a leather thong with a peculiar pouch hanging down from it.

'Aha!' he said when he opened the door. 'Come in, and welcome one and all! Evie – you need some colour in your cheeks. Paul – you and Evie should come here more often and get a spot of country air. Sean – you've grown so big you're a stranger to me! And, Leo –' Grandad turned towards him from hugging Sean.

Suddenly he became very still.

It was a stillness you could almost hear. Leo had the idea that everything had stopped. Grandad's hand had stopped in mid air; the hall clock had stopped swinging on its pendulum and Grandad's eyes had turned like leaves from yellow to an opaque gold.

'Leo,' he said, and his voice was rich as Christmas pudding, 'I've so looked forward to seeing you here.'

After that the day clicked on again. Leo's dad took the cases upstairs and

Sean started yelling to be outside. 'I want to be an Indian and hide in the trees and shoot anyone who passes by!'

Grandad said, 'Let him go now, Evie – he can't get up to much harm out there.'

Leo roamed around the house. First the living-room with its over-stuffed chairs; then the dining-room with its big French doors and sideboard full of silver plate. The kitchen stuck out at the back like a finger and musty blinds shut out the light. Each of the rooms that Leo went into was dark and full of moving shadows where the trees outside leaned over the sun. Even the conservatory was dark and the plants inside it smelled stale and musty, as if they needed watering. Leo caught himself thinking that Grandad's splendour had somehow sopped up all of the light, and that if he stayed in his house too long, then maybe he would begin to fade too.

He wandered back into the hall. Next to the hatstand there was another door, more imposing than the others. A door with a huge brass knob in the middle. When he touched the knob Leo heard a noise like the sea or dry grass swishing. He tried to take his hand away, but the knob seemed branded to his skin; there was a fierce burning that did not hurt but was more like a remembered pain. Behind him the hall was empty and dark. It was very quiet. He could not hear Sean whooping outside or his dad's voice

rumbling upstairs. But something made
him catch his breath. A sudden pressure
or a nudge from behind.

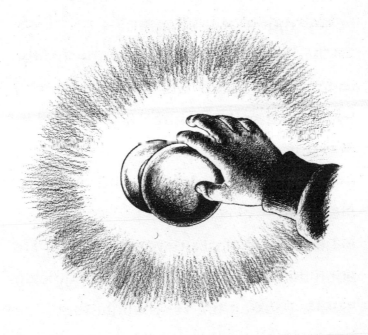

And, abruptly, Leo was inside the room.
Going from darkness into light.

At first Leo thought that the lights were on, or that the sun had mysteriously got through the roof. Or that Grandad's study had suddenly caught fire. But then he saw that it was a lion.

The lion stood to the right of the window. His head was on a level with Leo's head and his mane flamed gold in the stuffy gloom. Golden fire sparked from his pelt and dazzled outwards into the room.

Leo moved closer towards the lion. He put a hand out to touch him, then quickly drew it back again. He thought that if he touched the lion his hand would fizz and snap like a sparkler; that the lion would not let him go.

Leo put his hands behind his back. In
the pit of his stomach there was a sick sort
of feeling, and his eyes felt swollen as if he
might cry. He looked away. Then he
turned and looked into the lion's eyes.

This was *his* lion, he was sure of it. This

was the lion Leo saw every day; the lion from the picture on his bedroom wall, only more powerful and dangerous; more glorious than Leo had ever seen him before. His body was lean and muscular, his teeth were white and strong. His mouth was open to a black velvet hollow, as if he was trying to say something.

But Leo saw that this lion was dead.

Between his eyes there was a small, neat hole.

'You've found our lion, then? I knew you would.'

Grandad's rich, dark voice again, speaking to Leo very soft and low. Leo had not heard him come into the room, but the lion seemed suddenly to fade a little.

'Did you kill him?' Before he could speak to Grandad again, Leo had to know.

And for a long moment Grandad did not answer. Leo could sense him standing close behind; a strong, sweet smell crept over towards him, like parched earth before the summer rain. Then Grandad turned Leo round to face him. 'No, Leo,' he said, 'I did not. I have never killed a living thing – not knowingly at any rate. My father – your great-grandad – killed this lion, and that was many years ago.'

Leo said angrily, 'Well why do you keep him here, in this room? Why do you keep him where he doesn't belong?'

Grandad gave Leo a curious look.

Then he stroked the black leather pouch round his throat and said very slowly, 'Well now, Leo, what can I tell you in answer to that? Would you believe me if I said that I *don't* keep this lion? That – for the moment, at least – it's he who keeps me?'

Leo shrugged his shoulders and moved

away. Grandad was speaking in riddles, and the lion and the dark house seemed suddenly too strange and sad. He said, 'I'm going outside with Sean for a bit.'

'You do that, Leo – but remember, will you, you're a special person. You're different from Sean and the other lads. You're like me and your great-grandad. You're one of us.'

3 The African lion

FOR THE REST of the day Leo stayed outside. But even Sean's teasing and the gloomy garden with its restless trees could not take his mind off the lion. His thoughts kept going back into the room, back to the study where the lion was. He could see the lion in his mind's eye and feel the heat fizzing up from its coat. In the end he decided to go to bed early.

'What's the matter, Leo? Feeling tired?' His dad spoke up from behind his paper.

His mum said kindly, 'I'm tired myself. It's been that sort of a day for all of us.' She gave Leo her biggest smile.

Sean said, 'Well I think Leo's just being stupid – fancy wanting to go to bed *now*!'

Grandad stared at Leo from across the room. Then he put a finger to the side of his nose and tapped it very gently, 'Night, Leo, old lad,' he said.

Leo went to bed, but he could not sleep. He heard his family say goodnight and saw the last of the lights go off. Noises crept through the open window; he heard his dad cough in the next room.

After a while Leo got out of bed. The night air felt soft, like a silken breath which wrapped itself round him,

cocooning him from head to foot. There was the peculiar sensation of being drawn along; of being gently pulled out of his room and across the darkened landing, of going down the polished stairs, over the battered Turkish rug and along the passage to the lion's room.

When he touched the knob the door flew open and a stream of light came tumbling out. Leo knew that the lion was waiting for him, and that he was holding the swirling darkness back.

The lion glittered. Golden sparks flew off his coat, and a strong, sweet smell hung in the air. Leo looked at the lion's golden face. He thought he heard a soft, deep roar, or that the roar was the sound

of his own heart beating soft, then loud.
And then much louder. He stretched out a
hand and touched the lion, and at once
his skin began to snap and fizz. Pins and
needles ran up his arm. Leo could not
take his hand away from the lion. He
opened his mouth to give a shout and the
roar in his head came soaring out:

Roar! Roar! ROAR!

When the roar stopped the air was quiet. There was just the click of shadeless grass and the thump of the lion's heart in his chest. He flexed his paws in the thick silence and gazed up at the sprawling sky. Not a breath of wind ruffled his mane. A panting stillness made the heat a blue haze. This was December's hottest time and the lion stretched out beneath the sun. His belly was full. There was no need to kill. There was nothing to do but watch light move silently over the African plain.

When darkness dropped the lion stood up. The night air crawled with wild scents and the rustle of secret creatures. The lion

threw out his deep, broad chest and raised his head to the plush, black sky. His roar reached some hunters a few kilometres away. It woke them where they slept in their tents, and one of them made to reach for his gun . . .

Roar! Roar! ROAR!

'Leo! Leo! What's the matter? Have you got a pain or is it a dream?'

Leo was back in his bed, but he could not remember getting there. He could only remember the lion's roar, and the idea that he had been somewhere else. Somewhere hot and vast and wild. Inside his chest his heart was thumping and the thump made a roaring noise in his ears.

'You were shouting, Leo – or yelling, more like. You were making a really funny noise – whatever were you dreaming about?' Leo's mum put a hand on his forehead and stroked it gently. 'Whatever it was, it's made you hot. Get yourself up, Leo, and come downstairs and I'll make us all a nice pot of tea.'

Leo got out of bed and went to the window. Now that he was standing up he felt fitter and stronger than he usually did. Outside the window the sun was shining and Sean was already whooping about: '*Waah*! I'm a Red Indian, that's what I am! *Waah*! *Waah*! *Waah*!'

The rest of the family were downstairs in the kitchen. His dad was reading the paper again, his mum was eating a slice of toast, his grandad was at the kitchen sink.

When Leo opened the door Grandad turned round briefly and glanced at him. And just for a second Leo thought he saw something: a yellow spark in Grandad's eyes that flickered once and disappeared. Grandad said to him heartily, 'Well, you're looking chipper this morning, old lad – must be the special air round here.'

His mum said, 'I'd forgotten how

special this place is – it always makes me feel extra-well. I loved it here when I was a child.'

After breakfast they went for a walk through the woods. The sun was shining from a hard blue sky and tree shadows striped the summer grass.

Leo's mum said, 'I wish we could come and live here for good.'

His dad said, 'Remember how cold the winters are – and, anyway, what would we do about work?'

Leo walked slowly, enjoying the quiet and the flowers dotting the sides of the path. He walked so slowly he got left behind; his mum and dad disappeared from view and there was just the faint noise of Sean shouting and a bird twittering high above in the trees.

And then the sound of something panting. A dog or a fox or maybe a deer. Something that wasn't a human being.

Leo stopped walking. He turned round and scanned the path, but nothing and nobody was there. He set off again and quickened his pace. Ahead of him was a clearing in the woods made by loggers the previous year. Sunshine flooded it like light on a stage; it turned the green grass into silver and gold. But the clearing was empty of living creatures.

And then the sound came back again: *Pant. Pant. Pant.*

A hot lick of breath as fine as silk

tickled the side of Leo's face and cooled the glare of the midday heat. There was the notion again that something very soft and powerful had wrapped itself round him, that he was somehow cocooned in invisible silk. Then a twig nearby gave a sudden snap and Leo jumped and stood stock-still.

In front of him a lion appeared, padding slowly into the clearing, his mane standing out like a ruff of fire. The

lion was silent and sad-looking. His coat gave off a transparent glow.

A thin grey cloud wafted over the sun and Leo saw that the lion was really a man. A man who was walking slowly towards him; whose beard and hair made a silver ruff.

'Grandad!' yelled Leo.

Grandad waved his stick and kept on walking very slowly across the grass. Leo walked on to join the others. He could hear his mum saying, 'Where's Leo got to? Have you seen him, Sean?'

And Sean saying, 'Naah. I expect he's looking at some stupid flower.'

He saw his grandad pad towards them exactly like an ordinary man: he had a man's two arms, two legs, and a head; a proper man's nose and eyes and mouth.

Maybe the shadows had been playing tricks, or the sun had got into Leo's eyes – but in the clearing Grandad hadn't looked like a man. He had looked like something splendid and wild.

He had looked for all the world like a lion.

4 **Great-grandad**

AFTER TEA THAT day Leo went outside. Sean was upstairs playing Little Green Men. He had made his bed into a giant spaceship with the covers heaped up in the middle. When Leo went past he yelled at him, 'Come and play with me and be a spaceman and I'll be one of the Little Green Men.'

But Leo wanted to be by himself. He

kept on walking and he heard Sean say, 'You never play with me any more and there's no one else to play with here – you can be Captain if you like – or the Most Important Little Green Man.'

Leo went downstairs, out of the door and into the garden with its jungly trees and the stream running down the middle of it. He walked to the bridge that went over the stream and stared into the water. The trees at the side made zebra shadows zigzagged over with strips of light, and there was a smell of thick green vegetation. Then another smell on top of that. Wafting through the jungly trees.

Light but strong. A dry-grass smell that didn't belong in the damp, green shade of Grandad's wood.

Then, from behind him, Grandad said, 'There's something I want to show you, Leo, when you go back to the house. And it's private, OK? Just between you and me for the moment. No need to mention it to Sean.'

Leo jumped and turned round. Grandad was standing with his back to the house and the tree-shadows made a black mask of his face.

'What is it?' Leo asked. He felt shy with Grandad when he was on his own. He kept thinking of things he wanted to ask – all the things he had thought of at home – but the grandad in front of him was strange and alarming. He had a habit of appearing suddenly: in the study, in the woods, and now down by the stream at dusk. It was almost as if Grandad was stalking him. You never actually heard him arrive. He just appeared abruptly out of the blue.

Grandad said, 'Nothing to worry yourself about. Just some photos you might like to see. Some pictures taken in Africa when I was just a lad – that's what you wanted to know about, right? Come in when you're ready and we'll have a look.'

Leo stayed by the stream until the light was gone and small noises muttered and shushed in the dark. Then he went to Grandad's study and pushed at the heavy door. There was a creaking noise and the door came open. Inside, Grandad held a large brass key. He locked the door behind them.

'This place is private,' he said to Leo. 'There's things in here that are special to me and, maybe, one day they'll be special to you.' He fingered the black pouch round his neck, then gestured to Leo to come to his desk. On the desk there was a pile of photographs.

'This is me when I was a lad.' Grandad held out a photograph of a boy wearing baggy shorts and a floppy hat. The boy was clutching a long, sharp spear. 'The spear was only for show, d'you see. It was a present from one of the local men to my father when he was still just a lad. The locals call it an *assagai*. It is a sort of reward for becoming a man. They give it to you when you kill your first lion.'

The next picture showed a group of men with rifles over their arms. On the ground in front of them was the dead lion. Some of the men had a foot on it, and all of them were looking very proud.

Leo stared at the photograph. When he looked at it properly the men with the rifles seemed to fade away, so that all he could see was the lion.

'It's not our lion,' said Grandad softly. 'I expect you realised that straight away.'

Leo nodded. The men in the photograph made his skin feel cold and pinched. And when he looked at *their* lion standing beside the open window, he thought that it looked greyer and thinner than it had looked before. Or maybe it was Grandad again, sopping up all the light and power.

'And this is my father when he was young.' Grandad put a small photograph into Leo's hands. The picture had faded

to a smudgy brown, but the boy in it
looked familiar. He was small, with skinny
arms and legs and a
grin that was
oddly lopsided.
And, just for a
moment, Leo felt
rather strange. Like
he was looking at a picture of himself, a
picture that made him into a ghost.
Goose-pimples rippled over his skin. The
boy in the photograph looked familiar
because he looked exactly like Leo.

'I said you were a chip off the Leopold
block.' Grandad took the picture away
from Leo and put another one in his
hand. 'This is my father when he was

grown up.'

The next picture showed a fine, tall man. He was standing with the light behind him and the sun made a halo of his hair.

'He looks sad,' said Leo. He thought that the man's mouth was smiling brightly but his eyes were like two dark, empty pools.

'Yes,' said Grandad, 'I daresay he does. We'll come to that another day. But for now, young Leo, it's time you were off. Your mum will be wondering where you are. And, Leo – just remember, will you, that one day you'll be a fine young man, and that the best things take a bit of time to grow.'

Leo went to the door, and stopped for a

second. He turned round and waited, hesitating, then said, 'What happened to your father in the end?'

Grandad carried on stacking the photos together and there was a gap when he didn't say anything. Leo thought he heard a roar, faint as a distant thunderstorm. Darkness crept through the open window and the lion in the corner swelled and flashed.

'Storm's on its way,' Grandad said, 'and as to my father – well, young man. That's something that can wait for the moment.'

Later, Leo went to bed. It was very warm, and a long way off the storm grizzled and growled and shot out sparks of silvery light. The storm didn't get close to Grandad's house, but the noise of it made Leo restless. He tried to sleep, but the sound of the thunder got inside his head and changed from a growl to a roar. Low and insistent: *roar, roar*. The roar pulled Leo out of his bed. It wrapped him in its wild breath and sucked him down to the hall.

The study door stood slightly open, and there was a golden glow of luminous light which flowed from the study into the hall. Leo felt himself pulled by the silken breath, close to where the lion stood. Around the lion the air rumbled and heaved, and Leo put out a hand to touch its coat. As soon as he touched it his hand snapped and burned. Leo found that he was breathing very deeply, and that the breath was turning into a growl and the growl was turning into a –

ROAR!

The lion was very thirsty. It had been many months since the last fall of rain, and food and water were hard to find. In the dry shade he could hear his belly grumbling. Insects flicked in front of his eyes and clouds swelled and deflated and drifted by.

In the dreaming quiet the lion lay down, but he could not find sleep when he wanted to. A strange scent pricked at the back of his nose. Then a sound was

picked up and lost again.

And, instead of sleeping, the lion stood up. He sniffed the air and scanned the clouds and turned his head towards the plain. But everything was dead still and quiet. Nothing stirred or made a noise. The peculiar scent did not return. The lion gave a growl deep in his throat, and the growl was a threat and a warning. Nothing came back to answer the growl; the day slumped back to a fidgety quiet; hot, white sun glared down from the sky.

But still the lion could not settle down.

Something was not as it ought to be. There was danger somewhere he could not see or smell, and he knew it was getting closer.

The lion's growl changed to a mighty roar and he waited under the huge, white sky, sleepless, for the day to pass.

Leo was back in bed. He was hungry and frightened and puzzled as well. For the second time he thought that he had been somewhere else – possibly in Grandad's study – but surely Grandad kept it locked? And Leo did not know what he was frightened of. The storm had stopped and the moon was up; his room looked very peaceful and calm. But Leo's heart felt heavy and sad. He wished that the night would go away. He even wished that Sean was there.

But everybody slept except for Leo. He stared at the window with the moon behind it, making a pattern on the wall.

He thought that something bad had happened, or that something bad was *going* to happen.

And that it was something to do with their special lion.

5 **Hunters**

ALL THE NEXT day Leo felt sad. He did not want to go for a walk with the others. He did not want to play with Sean.

'But I'm fed up of playing on my own.' Sean was pulling the heads off dandelion clocks and looking at Leo as if he was seeing someone he didn't quite know. 'You haven't played with me once this week. If you want to we can play at lions and tigers – I'll be the tiger and you can be the lion.'

Leo shook his head. 'I'll play with you tomorrow.'

His mum looked up from her chair on the lawn. She was sitting with a book open on her knee, and she put a finger in it to keep the place. 'What's the matter, Leo?' she asked him kindly. 'I thought you'd like to be in the country, but you've been a bit down ever since we arrived.'

'I expect it's just the change of air,' Grandad answered Leo's mum before he could answer her himself. 'It's softer round here than it is up north. I expect that Leo's just feeling tired.' Grandad was speaking to Leo's mum, but all the time he was looking closely at Leo. And the expression on his face was serious and watchful, rather like a large guard dog. Grandad looked almost as if he was protecting Leo. His eyes seemed to follow him wherever he went, and if Leo went down the path to the woods he could hear the pad of Grandad's feet and smell his peculiar dry-grass smell.

Leo could not settle down all day. He walked round the garden and through the trees; he followed the stream to where it disappeared into a hole in the boggy ground. But shadows made him feel jumpy and scared. His heart felt heavy inside his chest and Leo kept thinking about the lion: the lion on his bedroom wall at home, the lion in the study and the lion on the plain. He was sure that somehow they were all the same lion.

That night when Leo went to bed, Grandad said, 'God bless, old son – and take good care.'

Leo's mum said, 'There's not a lot he can get up to, Dad – not when he's safely tucked up in bed.'

And Grandad gave a laugh that did not sound happy, while his eyes followed Leo to the living-room door.

Upstairs in his room Leo opened the window and leaned out as far as he could. Behind him the moon made a path to the door. Leo waited until his mum and dad went to bed, then he went outside to the cool, dark landing. He waited to feel the lion's breath, but instead of a silky, soft cocoon, there was just the empty dark of the house and the hollow well of the oaken stairs.

Very quietly Leo went down the stairs . . .

Along the passage to the study door . . .

The door was closed but, when Leo touched it, his hand felt tingly. He gave it a push and straight away the door swung open, and Leo stepped into the room.

The lion was waiting.

His mouth open to a black velvet hole.

Leo thought he could see the lion breathe, and that with each deep ingoing breath the lion was drawing him closer towards the golden pelt, until Leo could feel the heat from the lion huffing against his own cold skin. He could hear the crack of electricity running over the sparking fur, and he could smell the peculiar dry-grass smell over the fusty smell of the room.

Very carefully, Leo put out his hand.

As soon as he touched the lion's fur his skin began to throb and burn. His heart began to beat with the lion's heart: soft, then loud, then louder still, until the heartbeat was a thud in Leo's ears and the breaths he took were the lion's own. They made a rattling noise in his chest, and the rattle became a long, low, growl,

Gro-owl, Gro-owl! GRO-OWL . . .

Under the fierce, unquenchable sun, each day was the same as the one before: no food, no rain, no deep, cool shade. Just the rumble of an empty belly and the circling of vultures overhead.

The lion lay down on the thin, dry earth and let the weight of his head drop down. He could feel the force of each short breath rasping in and out of his chest. He could hear the whirr of the vultures' wings and the buzz of a fly diving on to his pelt.

Then came a noise he hadn't heard before. A sudden click that wasn't grass. A scent that wasn't a scent he knew. But nothing moved across the plain; no strange animal came into view. There was just an awareness of something wrong; something dangerous and unknown.

With a sudden movement the lion stood up. He opened his mouth to give a roar. But the smell became stronger all at once.

There was a sudden sense of darkness coming. Then the click became an explosion of noise.

'*Bang*!' cried Leo. '*Bang*! *Bang*! *Bang*!'

In the study it suddenly went very dark. Leo could not see the lion clearly, or Grandad's desk, or the pictures on the wall. The darkness was very still and quiet. No light came from the lion's coat, and Leo's hand on its fur felt stiff and cold.

For a long while Leo stayed where he was. Through the open window he could feel the night's cool breeze on his face. Then came small, wild sounds from the woods: the hoot of an owl and some leaves rustling. Gently Leo took his hand away from the lion. He felt sad again, and very tired. His heart was heavier than it had ever been – too heavy for his chest, Leo thought.

He looked at the lion through the gloom, and what he saw was just a lion. A lion with dark and shabby fur. No spark came from the lion's eyes; his fur didn't snap or crack with light.

Leo put his hand back on the lion's cool pelt. He stroked the fur very slowly and sadly, then turned and moved towards the door.

But in the hall there was the dry-grass smell.

A strange, hot scent that tickled his nose.

And Leo thought he saw the shape of a lion slowly padding up the stairs. He caught his breath and waited a moment, then followed after the shadow-lion. But, when he got to the landing, nothing was there except for the ghostly shape of a picture outlined dimly against the wall.

Leo went to his room and closed the door. In his heart he knew that the lion was dead, and that Grandad knew what had happened to it. But Grandad was keeping the truth to himself, and Leo was fretful and unsure. He knew that the lion was more than a lion who was simply special to them. The lion had a power that was unique: he was something to do with who Grandad was.

Leo closed his eyes and the lion appeared, and his face was a flaming blaze of light, and his mane was a flaming blaze of gold.

6 **Lionheart**

T HE SUN WAS shining in the morning. Leo felt it first on his eyes and then on his nose. When he opened his eyes the room was full of rippling light moving in and out of the trees.

He sat up in bed, and maybe it was the

sun shining through the window that made Leo feel so strong and happy. When he got out of bed he felt taller than usual, and his arms and legs felt springy and light. Leo had a wash and brushed his teeth and went to the mirror to comb his hair. His skin seemed brighter than it had the day before, and the hair round his face was a golden fuzz that snapped and cracked when he tugged the comb through it.

As soon as he was ready Leo went downstairs. His mum was in the kitchen eating toast. She glanced up idly when Leo walked in, and paused with the toast halfway to her mouth. 'Goodness, Leo, you look well this morning. I think your face has caught the sun – it's gone a lovely dark-gold shade, and the sun's made your hair a bit lighter too.'

His grandad said, 'I think Leo's at home here now. I think he feels that he really belongs.' And his voice was purry like a cat's.

'He's starting to look a lot like you.' That was Leo's dad speaking out. He looked at Leo as if he was surprised. 'He's got the same sort of face and hair. He'll be the spitting image of you when he grows up.'

'I told you he was a chip off the Leopold block.' Grandad was smiling at Leo across the table, and Leo saw with astonishment that they *did* look alike. And Grandad's father had looked like

Grandad. So that made three Leopold's in a row, each looking very much like the last.

Then Sean said, 'Well, I take after Dad so *there*. And I reckon Dad's much bigger than Grandad – or at least, he is when Grandad's sitting down.'

Everybody laughed and, after a minute, Sean laughed too. He said to Leo, 'Are you going to play with me today? We can play at outlaws in the woods and I'll be the outlaw and you can hunt me down.'

And just for an instant Leo heard himself growl very softly, and a golden spark flashed in front of his eyes. Then he surprised himself by saying, 'No – I don't like playing at hunting now. We'll play at being sailors instead – I'll be the captain and you can be the crew.'

After breakfast the others went outside – all except for Grandad who said, 'Come with me to the study, Leo? There's something we need to talk about.'

Leo followed his grandad down the hall and in through the heavy wooden door. And immediately he saw that the lion was gone.

'He's in the attic,' Grandad said, following the direction of Leo's eyes. 'I don't think we need him here for a while – don't you worry, he's well wrapped up, the moths won't get into our special lion.'

Then Grandad sat down at his desk.

He pulled open a drawer and took a photograph out of it. For a long moment he studied the photograph, and Leo thought that while he was doing it, some of the brightness went out of him, rather like a flame that has burned down.

Finally, with a sigh, he handed the picture to Leo. 'This is our lion,' he said. 'My father (your great-grandfather) stalked it for months, all through the spring-time plenty, up until the terrible drought. He got to know the lion almost like a kindred spirit – a creature who was free and wild; who lived off the land and did what he liked, who answered to no one but himself.

'Except, of course, that my father *did*

answer to someone. He answered to the people who employed him to take them out and hunt the game. And a lion was always the most prized of creatures. You were someone in those days if you killed a lion. But your great-grandad never meant to kill him.'

Grandad sighed again, and rubbed a hand through his silver hair. 'One day he was out with a party of hunters and one of the party spotted the lion. *Our* lion, who was pretty thin by then. There'd been no rain to speak of for months, you see, and most of the animals were thin and starved – but there was always the chance the rains would come and the strongest animals would be saved. And our lion was young and fit and strong . . .

'But he was spotted by a man who shouldn't have had a gun because he could never shoot straight. He'd wound a creature and not kill it out-right, and then my father would have to finish it off.

'So this man spots our special lion and, before my father could take his gun, he had it lined up in his sights, and my father had to act quickly or else . . . the other man would have wounded it . . .

'D'you see, old son? Why he *had* to do it? My father had to shoot that lion or the other bloke would have bodged the job. So he pulled the trigger when the lion turned and, for one split second, looked into its eyes. Then the gun went off with a mighty *bang*! – and that's when a really strange thing occurred.

'He pulled the trigger and the lion dropped down, and straight away my father felt this pain. Not in the head where he shot the lion, but in his heart where he felt a terrible jolt. Then darkness swirled into his brain, so black it made him drop to the ground. When it cleared he understood what had happened – that the heart had gone out of him for good. And, Leo . . . ' Grandad leaned in close, 'he knew it had gone straight into the lion.'

7 The Leopold line

LEO CAUGHT HIS breath, and Grandad paused for a moment. Then he smiled at Leo; a slow, sweet smile that lit up his face. Leo smiled back, and Grandad said, 'My father took the lion home – but, like I told you, the heart had gone out of him. You hardly ever saw him smile after that, and his eyes had a brooding, inward look, as if he was staring at things no one else could see. He never shot an animal again. Instead he founded a sanctuary (and that was unusual at the time) so that the animals who lived in it would be safe from hunters while they were there. They called the sanctuary "Simba", which was the local word for lion – and that's where father stayed and worked for the rest of his long life.

'Only . . . in spite of all the hard work he did, there was a dark spot at the heart of him, and he never forgot his special lion.

'But then my mother had *me*. And I always felt this pull towards lions – I was never so happy as when I was with them. When I got to be your age, I found the door to my father's study left open. And that's when I touched the special lion and felt the lion's heart give a jump – and that's when I felt the heart beat inside me, and the lion's strength seep into my bones.

'And that heart goes from one to the other of us – down the line of Leopolds – from my father to the lion, from the lion to me – and now, Leo, it has gone into you – or some of it at any rate. I've still got some use for it at the moment, so you'll have to wait your turn for the full lion-power.'

Grandad stopped talking and Leo stayed quiet. But inside his head he was picturing things; he was roaring at the teacher who made him look silly, and at Kevin Phipps for stealing his lunch. He was roaring at Sean for calling him small. In his head Leo was tossing his mane and swishing his tail and rampaging across the playground at school, and no other creature dared cross his path because Leo was lord of all that he surveyed.

Grandad spoke again. He had been watching Leo, and he seemed to know

what Leo was thinking, because he said softly, 'It doesn't work like that, you know. Being strong means being careful of other creatures – that's what my father found out too late, and that's why he was always so sad. You have to be strong to be a lion, but you have to be kind and fair as well.

'And now, Leo, there's one more thing.' Grandad fumbled at his throat where the leather pouch was. He opened the drawstring at the neck of the pouch and took out an object which he held in his hand. Gently he took Leo's hand in his. 'This is the bullet which killed the lion.' Grandad pressed a small, hard piece of metal into Leo's hand. And, immediately,

Leo's skin went cold and his heart began to beat slowly and heavily. When Leo put out his hand to give Grandad the bullet back, his hand and arm were heavy and weighted, as if the strength was oozing out of them.

Grandad said, 'My father kept this with him all his life. It was a kind of symbol of what had happened. He reckoned that if the bullet got lost, then the Leopold line would just die out – but don't you worry about that just yet. I simply wanted you to know that it's rightfully yours, so that when the time comes and you're strong enough, the bullet will finish up where it belongs.'

Leo watched Grandad put the bullet away. As soon as it was out of his hands he felt lighter and happier. Then a thought struck him. 'Why were you following me around? You were in the wood and by the stream – why did you have to keep track of me?'

Grandad leaned forward and looked closely into Leo's face. And the dry-grass smell came back again. In the dark study Leo glimpsed a wide blue sky; he heard the drum-beat of his heart and felt the hot sun on his skin. Then Grandad spoke in his chocolate voice, rich and brown and velvety. 'The lion's power is very strong – stronger than you can ever know. And you're young yet, Leo, so I had to take care. I had to make sure you were safe from the lion.'

Leo went outside. In the garden the sun was shining, but in spite of the warmth coming from it, Leo shivered.

'What's the matter, Leo? Somebody just walked over your grave?'

Leo's dad was teasing him, but he still made Leo jump. The sun was making his dad feel warm, but to Leo it felt weak and thin. He decided that when he grew up he would go to Africa where the sun really burned; he would feel the same heat that the lion felt, he might even walk the same tracks as the lion. In the meantime his dad was looking at him. And Leo shrugged his shoulders nonchalantly. He said, 'I just thought about something, Dad, that's all. When I grow up I'll be a vet – and maybe I'll go and work with lions.'

8 **Roar!**

TWO WEEKS LATER they were back at home and Sean was making his usual noise.

'*Vroom*! I'm a fighter plane. *Ack-ack-ack*! Watch out, Leo, or I'll shoot you down!'

Leo felt a push when Sean went past, and immediately a spark went *flash*! and Leo saw a yellow streak of light. He felt a snarl start deep in his throat – but then he remembered what Grandad said: *You have to be strong to be a lion, but you have to be kind and fair as well.*

He put his hands inside his pockets and went to the door of the living-room. Sean stopped being a plane and followed him. He said, 'You can be the one to shoot *me* if you like.' Sean's voice was smaller and quieter than it usually was.

After a minute Leo said back, 'Naah, it's all right. Let's go outside so we won't make a mess – then you can be the pilot and I'll be the crew.'

The next day Leo went back to school, and his teacher said to him straight away, 'My, Leo, you've certainly grown. That holiday must have suited you – you're taller, I'm sure, and your skin's gone gold.'

Then at lunch time Kevin Phipps came up. He stuck his red face close to Leo and said, 'Give us your lunch right now – *or else*!'

Leo thought of the lion and what his grandad said – the bit about being kind and fair. He stood up straight and threw back his head. He opened his mouth as far as he could, and out came a mighty, ear-splitting . . .

RO

AR!

If you enjoyed this
MAMMOTH READ try:

The Stare

Pat Moon
Illustrated by *Greg Gormley*

Jenna can't believe it – just by staring
at someone she can make them do
whatever she likes! The results are
hilarious – not to mention chaotic!

Her best friend, Eddie, thinks it's
the most amazing gift – Jenna really
is telepathic. Then he discovers
the secret behind Jenna's
new-found talent.

But when he tries to warn her, she
just won't listen . . .

If you enjoyed this
MAMMOTH READ try:

How's Harry?

Steve May
Illustrated by *Philip Hopman*

Harry's a hamster and Kate's going to
have him for a pet, whatever her parents
say. Her dad doesn't think she can look
after him properly – every five minutes
he asks, 'How's Harry?'

It drives Kate mad. All she wants
is to help Harry find happiness. But
when she asks Harry what he wants
from life, he can't tell her.

Kate decides she knows best.
She will take Harry back to his
roots . . . in the Syrian desert!